4/03

17. 99

RAYMOND BRIGGS

UG

BOY GENIUS OF THE STONE AGE AND HIS SEARCH FOR SOFT TROUSERS

ALFRED A. KNOPF
NEW YORK

For
TOM *"Why do they have trees?"* BENJAMIN,
CLARE, SARAH, CONNIE, MATILDA & MILES

THIS IS A BORZOI BOOK PUBLISHED BY ALFRED A. KNOPF

Copyright © 2001 by Raymond Briggs
All rights reserved under International and Pan-American Copyright Conventions. Published in the United
States of America by Alfred A. Knopf, a division of Random House, Inc., New York. Distributed by
Random House, Inc., New York.
Originally published in Great Britain by Jonathan Cape Ltd., a division of Random House UK, in 2001
KNOPF, BORZOI BOOKS, and the colophon are registered trademarks of Random House, Inc.

www.randomhouse.com/kids

Library of Congress Cataloging-in-Publication Data
Briggs, Raymond.
Ug : boy genius of the Stone Age / Raymond Briggs.
p.   cm.
Summary: To the dismay of his parents and friends, a prehistoric boy continually thinks of making things
softer, warmer, and nicer, rather than being content in a world of stone.
ISBN 0-375-81611-9 (trade) — ISBN 0-375-91611-3 (lib. bdg.)
[1. Prehistoric peoples—Fiction. 2. Stone age—Fiction. 3. Genius—Fiction. 4. Cartoons and comics.]
I. Title.
PZ7.B76433 Ug 2002
[Fic]—dc21   2001038102

First Borzoi Books edition: September 2002
Printed in Singapore
10 9 8 7 6 5 4 3 2 1

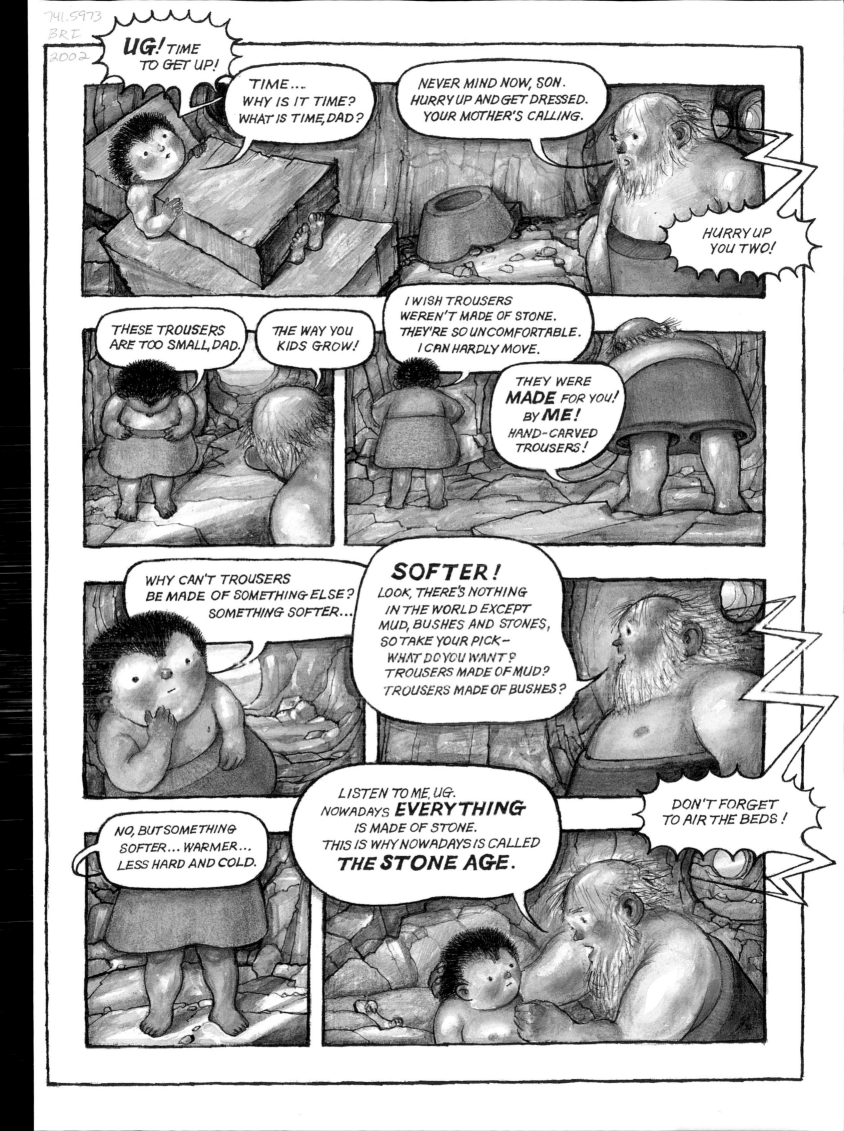

STONE AGE: (anachronism)
NO ONE LIVING IN
THE STONE AGE
WOULD KNOW HE WAS
LIVING IN THE STONE AGE.
HE WOULD BELIEVE HE WAS
LIVING IN THE MODERN AGE.
TODAY WE BELIEVE WE ARE
LIVING IN THE MODERN AGE.
    TIME WILL TELL.

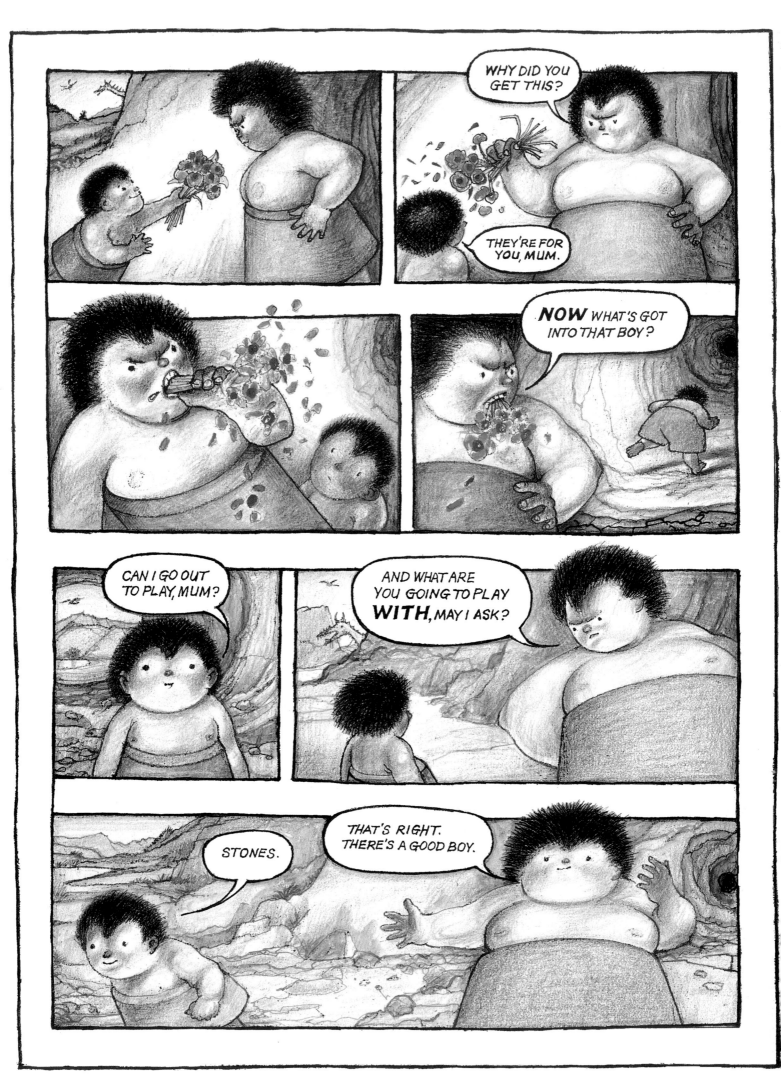

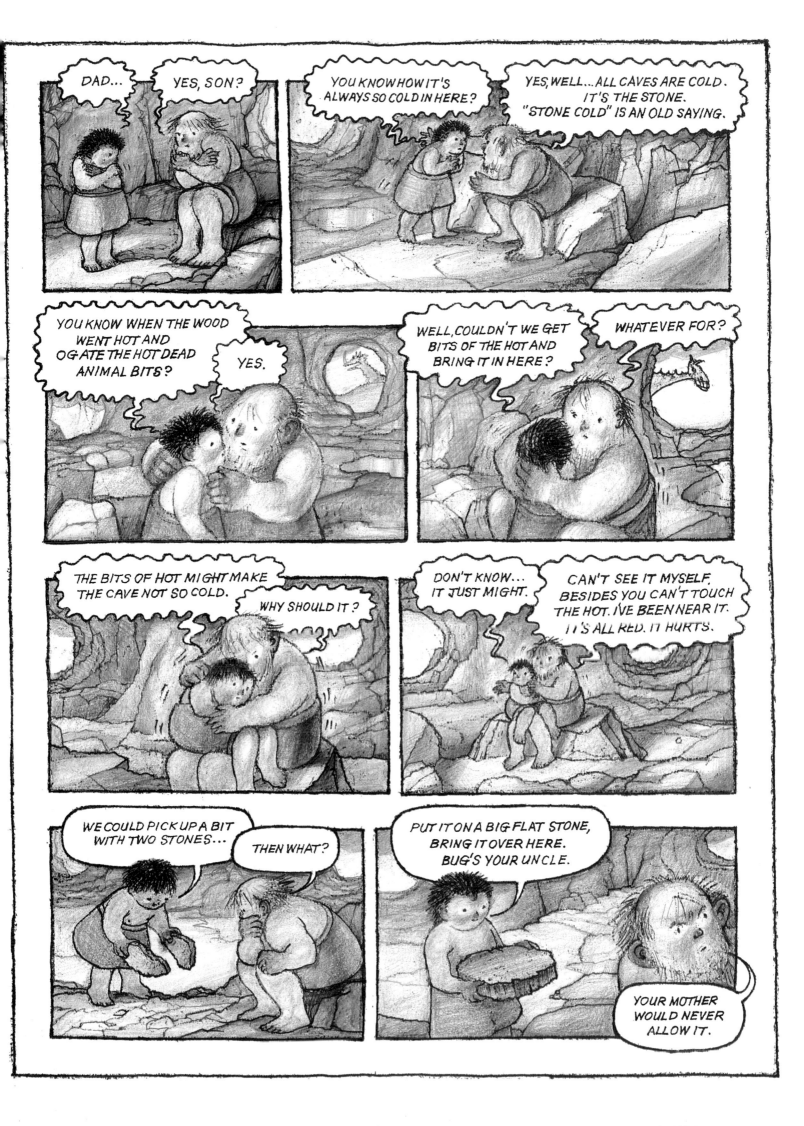

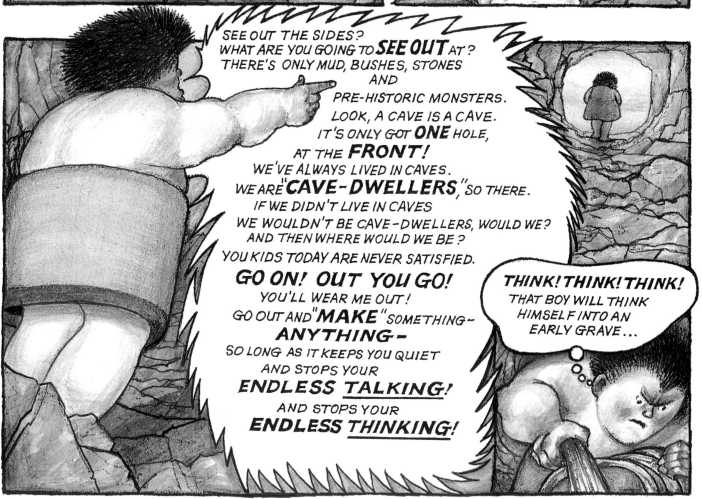

EVEN YOU MUST HAVE HEARD OF IT. IT'S FAMOUS. "THE LABORS OF SISYPHUS," IT'S CALLED. THE LABORS OF A LOONY MORE LIKE. I'M GOING TO BED. I CAN'T COPE WITH IT ANY MORE. DID YOU MAKE THE BED LIKE I TOLD YOU THIS MORNING?

I PUT THE BEDSTONE BACK ON TOP, DUGS.

THAT'S ALL RIGHT THEN. I HATE GOING IN THERE AND FINDING THE BED NOT MADE.

① WEEK: (anachronism)
THERE WERE NO "WEEKS" IN THE STONE AGE, NOR WERE THERE "MONTHS" OR "YEARS." IN THE STONE AGE, TIME STOOD STILL. THIS IS WHY SO LITTLE PROGRESS WAS MADE AND WHY IT TOOK AN AGE TO COME TO AN END.

② LUNCH: (possible anachronism)
IT IS NOT KNOWN FOR CERTAIN WHAT THE MIDDAY MEAL WAS CALLED IN THE STONE AGE.

③ SISYPHUS: (anachronism)
SISYPHUS CAME MUCH LATER, AFTER HISTORY STARTED. HE WAS A GREEK (OR A ROMAN) AGES AGO (POSSIBLY EVEN BC). HE PUSHED STONES UPHILL, LET THEM ROLL DOWN AGAIN, THEN PUSHED THEM UP AGAIN, LET THEM ROLL DOWN, PUSHED THEM UP AGAIN, LET THEM ROLL DOWN, THEN PUSHED THEM UP AGAIN. HE KEPT ON DOING IT FOR YEARS, OVER AND OVER AGAIN, FOR YEARS AND YEARS. HE BECAME FAMOUS FOR DOING IT.

② SUMMER HOLIDAY: (anachronism)
SUMMER HOLIDAYS WERE UNKNOWN
IN THE STONE AGE.
ALTHOUGH NO ONE WENT TO WORK,
THE STRUGGLE FOR SURVIVAL WAS SO HARD,
DUE TO THE STONY CONDITIONS, THE MUD
AND THE ENORMOUS NUMBER OF BUSHES
THAT THERE WAS LITTLE TIME LEFT
FOR HOLIDAYS. SO THEY WERE UNKNOWN.
  FURTHERMORE, THE CLIMATE WAS
COMPLETELY DIFFERENT TO THE PRESENT
DAY AND "SUMMER" WAS PROBABLY
UNKNOWN DUE TO THE CLIMATE
BEING COMPLETELY DIFFERENT.

③ BOOTS: (anachronism)
BOOTS WERE ALMOST UNKNOWN IN THE
STONE AGE. ANIMALS WITH LEATHERY
SKINS HAD NOT YET EVOLVED, AS ALL
THE ANIMALS WERE STILL PRE-HISTORIC
MONSTERS. SUCH BOOTS AS DID EXIST
WERE MADE OF STONE AND WERE
ALMOST AS UNCOMFORTABLE AS THE
STONE TROUSERS. SO THEY WERE NEVER
USED. CONSEQUENTLY, NO STONE AGE
BOOT HAS EVER BEEN FOUND, AND
OF COURSE, NEVER A PAIR.